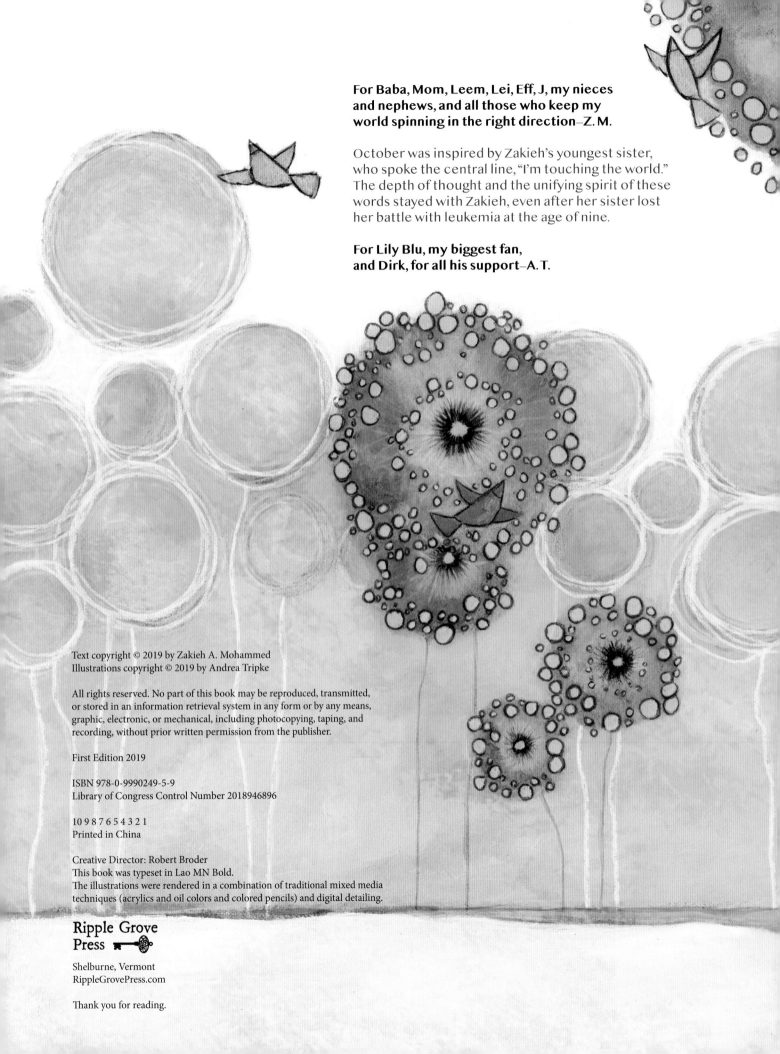

For Baba, Mom, Leem, Lei, Eff, J, my nieces
and nephews, and all those who keep my
world spinning in the right direction–Z. M.

October was inspired by Zakieh's youngest sister,
who spoke the central line, "I'm touching the world."
The depth of thought and the unifying spirit of these
words stayed with Zakieh, even after her sister lost
her battle with leukemia at the age of nine.

For Lily Blu, my biggest fan,
and Dirk, for all his support–A. T.

Text copyright © 2019 by Zakieh A. Mohammed
Illustrations copyright © 2019 by Andrea Tripke

First Edition 2019

ISBN 978-0-9990249-5-9
Library of Congress Control Number 2018946896

10 9 8 7 6 5 4 3 2 1
Printed in China

Creative Director: Robert Broder
This book was typeset in Lao MN Bold.
The illustrations were rendered in a combination of traditional mixed media
techniques (acrylics and oil colors and colored pencils) and digital detailing.

Ripple Grove
Press

Shelburne, Vermont
RippleGrovePress.com

Thank you for reading.

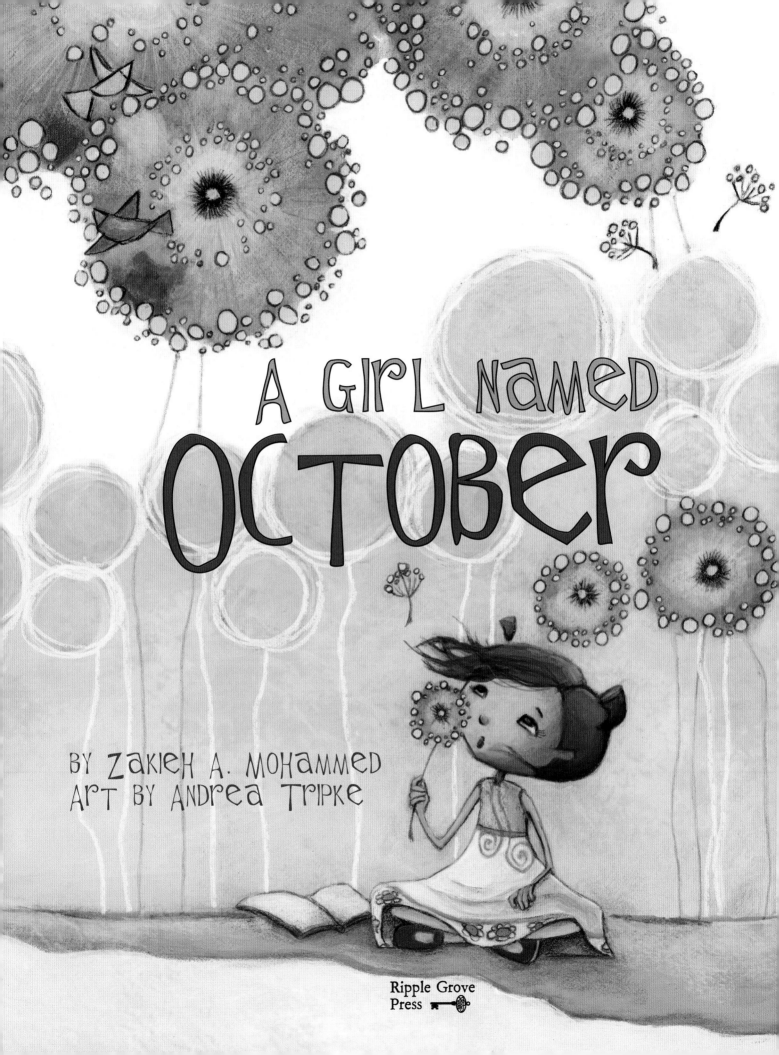

A GIRL NAMED OCTOBER

BY ZAKIEH A. MOHAMMED
ART BY ANDREA TRIPKE

Ripple Grove
Press

OCTOBER WAS A WISE, quiet girl
with long lashes of autumn wheat.

She often would stand looking at nothing
of which I could see.

"What are you doing?" I asked one day.

"I'm standing on the world," she responded with certainty.

Then, pointing at my feet, she asked,
"Aren't you?"

I did not know how to answer, so I said nothing.

Whenever I came across October, she always
had the corners of her lips curved upward.

"Why are you smiling?" I asked.

"I'm touching the world," she said, her world
seeming pleasant, calm, and full of purpose.
"There are so many ways, aren't there?"

I did not know how to answer, so I said nothing.

One weary day, my frustration led me to pick up a stone, and I threw it into the water.

I watched as it kissed the surface, sending out hundreds of ripples over the pond.

October strolled beside me and whispered, "You see it, don't you?"

I did not know how to answer, so I said nothing.

As I rushed about, on another occasion, I found October walking beside me with an armful of thick books.

"What are you going to do with all those books?" I asked.

October smiled, handing me one.
"When I read them, I can see farther. Can't you?"

I did not know how to answer, so I said nothing.

One dreary morning,
there was October in the window,
painting with a light touch on the paper
that picked up the
greens,
    yellows,
        and purples
that she swirled about the page.

I called to her and asked,
"Why are you painting?"

She handed the painting to me and said,
"So I can have longer arms.
Do you know how far you can reach?"

I did not know how to answer, so I said nothing.

Sometimes I would find October sitting on a crackled, old bench with a pen in her hand and a notebook in her lap.

She wrote words that were soft and peaceful, and sometimes sharp and really too truthful.

I asked, "Why are you writing those words?"

She answered with hands outstretched
like a century-old oak that wanted to
sweep the stars out of the sky.
"I speak loudly when I say nothing at all.
You heard me, didn't you?"

I did not know how to answer,
so I said nothing.

On a hot afternoon, I saw October running barefoot on the sandy shore as she tried to catch the breath of the wind on the sticky day.

She stopped at a shell that captured the sun in its opal face. Delicate ridges lived on the shell, and October rubbed them between her fingers. She smiled and then put it back on the beach.

I called out, "Why don't you keep it?"

She looked up with cheerful eyes. "But I did, didn't you?"

I did not know how to answer, so I said nothing.

A new season had come, and the dandelions had turned.
They were now stalks of snowflakes—light, dusty, and soft.

October held a strand and blew gently on the puffy, flecked
cotton ball. The specks caught the breath of October as they
scattered fearlessly.

October delighted in the dandelion fleece as though she were
blowing candles on her very own birthday cake.

I asked, "Why do you take the time?"

She smiled and said,
"My eyes are so much bigger when I do.
What great things have you seen?"

I did not know how to answer, so I said nothing.

A bad wind came one night,
and everything was tossed and turned,
and the sky was gray with worry.

Yet there was October,
skipping over dusty sidewalks
as though a carnival had come
and she would be the first one
on every ride.

I called out to her, "Why are you skipping?"

She stopped to remedy an overturned bicycle and said,
"Because my heart beats louder in a terrible storm,
doesn't yours?"

I did not know how to answer, so I said nothing.

Crisp leaves rustled under October's footsteps.
I watched her cool shadow stretch
to the tall oak;
the tall oak stretch its lean,
long branches to the blue jay;
and the roots of the oak sink
to the bottom of the earth.

I took a deep breath,
and I felt sad.

The sun settled down, and the wind whispered at first and then was quiet.

I was tired and had no answers.

I was older and heavier in my heart,
    in my step,
        and in my hope.

I tried to lift my head—my very heavy head—
and out of the corner of my eye I saw
long lashes of autumn wheat blowing in my direction.

October was smiling for me at this one moment
when I was too tired, and then I did understand.

October was touching the world,
and as I smiled back ...

I knew I was touching it too.